Snow White

and the Seven Dwarfs

Illustrated by Thai My Phuong

BONNEY
PRESS

Published by Bonney Press,
an imprint of Hinkler Books Pty Ltd
45–55 Fairchild Street
Heatherton Victoria 3202 Australia
www.hinkler.com.au

BONNEY
PRESS

© Hinkler Books Pty Ltd 2016

Illustration: Thai My Phuong
Text: Katie Hewat
Design: Paul Scott and Pooja Desai
Editorial: Emily Murray

ISBN: 978 1 4889 0485 1

Printed and bound in China

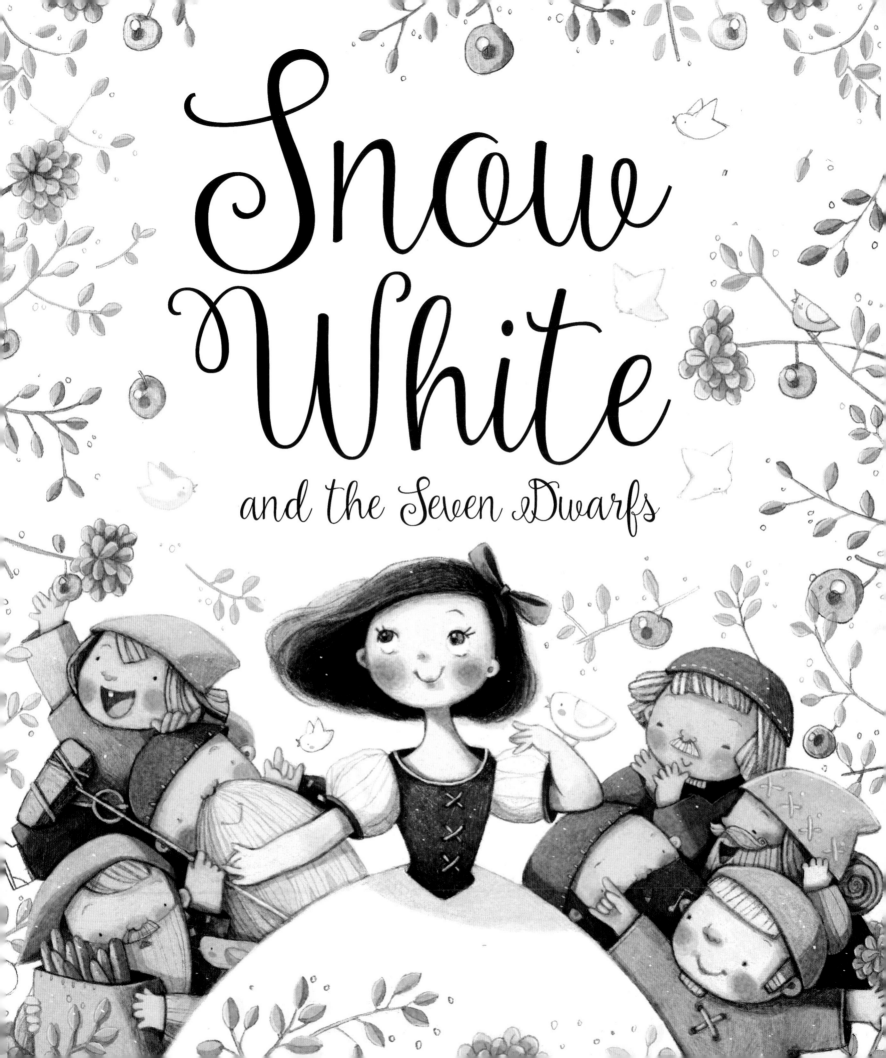

Snow White

and the Seven Dwarfs

Once upon a time there lived a princess named Snow White. She had skin as white as snow, lips as red as a rose and hair as **black** as ebony.

Snow White's stepmother, the queen, was also very beautiful, but very vain. She owned a magic mirror which always answered truthfully to any question it was asked.

The queen would often stand in front of the mirror combing her long hair and ask:

'Mirror, mirror, on the wall, Who is *fairest* of them all?'

And the mirror would sigh, wondering why nobody ever asked questions like, 'What is the meaning of life?' But it would reply,

'You are fairest of all.'

This made the queen *very* happy.

As Snow White grew up, she became even more beautiful. One morning, when the queen asked her question, the mirror replied, a little too cheerfully, *'Snow White is fairest of all.'* The queen flew into a terrible rage and called her trusted huntsman to her.

'I want Snow White **gone**!' she told him. 'Take her into the woods and tie her to a tree. She will be eaten by wild animals and never return.' The huntsman set off to do as he was told.

But when the huntsman took Snow White into the forest, and she happily chatted away and offered to carry his bow for him, he found he could not bring himself to do what the queen had ordered; so he let her go.

'Run away as far as you can, and never return,' he told Snow White. So she ran into the forest, and kept running for as long as she could.

Just as cold and hunger finally
set in, she saw a small cottage
in the distance. Finding nobody
at home, she gently opened the door
and went inside.

Inside the cottage, she found a *tiny* table with seven very small place settings. In the kitchen she found bread and water, which she savoured while sitting in a *tiny* chair.

The cottage was warm and comfortable, and Snow White was very tired, so she curled up on one of the seven *tiny* beds and was soon sleeping soundly.

When it was dark outside, the owners of the cottage came home. They were **seven dwarfs** who mined in the mountains for gold and silver.

The dwarfs carried their candles into the cottage and were very frightened by the **giant** they found asleep inside.

'What *is* it?'

'A monster!'

'What shall we do?'

'Attack it!'

'Wait, wait, wait,' said another. 'It's just a human girl.'

The dwarfs all crowded around Snow White to get a closer look.

'So it is. Silly us!'

Snow White awoke with a start to find seven little men standing around her. She was frightened at first but quickly realised the dwarfs were very friendly.

When Snow White told them her story, they soon became fast friends and the dwarfs decided that she should stay with them in their cottage.

'But you must be very careful,' one of the dwarfs warned her. 'You may still be in danger from the queen. So don't go out into the woods alone and never, ever open the door to a stranger.'

Back at the castle, the queen (believing that Snow White was no longer a problem) arose the next morning, went to her magic mirror and asked:

'Mirror, mirror, on the wall,
Who is *fairest* of them all?'

The mirror replied with a groan,

'Snow White is fairest of all.'

'That foolish huntsman! He can't even be trusted to get rid of a silly little girl! If you want something done right, you have to do it *yourself.'*

So the jealous queen, who was consumed with **anger**, decided she would not rest until she found where Snow White was hiding.

First, the queen began by plastering 'WANTED' posters in every town and along every roadside. But the creatures of the forest, who loved Snow White, made it their mission to tear each one down. After receiving no news of Snow White's whereabouts, the queen realised the answer had been right in front of her all along.

She stood before her magic mirror and asked:

'Mirror, mirror, oh so *fragile*,
Where has the **brat** been all this while?'

The mirror, feeling somewhat alarmed at the queen's angry tone and her ability to smash him into one hundred tiny pieces, sadly replied,

'Snow White lives with the seven dwarfs in their cottage in the forest.'

The queen set to work on an evil plan. Disguising herself as a peasant woman, she scoured the markets for the **biggest**, *juiciest* apples she could find. Then she selected the best apple of the bunch and carefully brushed one side with poison.

The queen then placed the apples in a basket and made her way
to the dwarfs' cottage.

Once there, she waited patiently for the dwarfs to go to work.

'Apples for sale!' called the queen outside the cottage window. Remembering the dwarfs' warning, Snow White cautiously peered out the window, and upon seeing the delicious apples in the basket, said sadly, 'I am not to let anyone in.'

'There is no need,' replied the queen, as she took a large bite from the un-poisoned side of the apple. 'Here, try this,' she said, and passed the apple through the window.

Snow White thought she'd much rather have her own apple rather than a germy, half-eaten one. But not wanting to be rude to the kind old lady, she took the apple and bit into the opposite side. The poison struck immediately and Snow White fell to the floor.

Delighted at her success, the queen cackled with laughter all the way back the castle.

As soon as she arrived, she went straight to her magic mirror.

This time, in answer to her question, the bored mirror answered,

You are fairest of all.

The queen was very pleased.

That evening, the dwarfs found Snow White lying on the cottage floor. Distraught, they tried *everything* they could think of to wake her, but nothing worked.

The dwarfs wanted her to be at peace, so they made Snow White a glass casket and took her into the woods where they could watch over her. Even the animals came to mourn for her.

One day, a *handsome* prince happened by the casket and was instantly mesmerised by the *beautiful* girl inside. He knew he could not live without being able to look upon her lovely face, so he asked the dwarfs for permission to take her back to his kingdom.

The dwarfs agreed, sad to lose Snow White, but glad that she would have a fine resting place.

The prince thanked the dwarfs, and began to ready the casket for the long journey. But as he lifted the casket, the piece of poisoned apple was freed from Snow White's mouth and she **instantly awoke.**

Snow White and the prince fell *madly in love*, and soon travelled to the prince's kingdom to be married.

They lived happily ever after, often returning to the cottage in the forest to visit their favourite friends, the dwarfs.

The queen, having believed this whole time that Snow White was gone, stood in front of her magic mirror one day and asked her favourite question. This time, the mirror gleefully answered:

'Evil queen, who art so vain,
Snow White is alive again.
She is lovely of heart and face,
And has a thousand times
your beauty and grace.'

And with that, the queen exploded in a puff of green, jealousy-filled smoke; never to be seen again.